SQUEAK!
SQUAWK!
ROAR!

With huge thanks to my brilliant and patient team at Otter-Barry Books and talented illustrator Hannah Asen for bringing *Squeak! Squawk! Roar!* alive, and also to all my kind, helpful supporters, online and on land, along the way!

To the animals inside - best behaviour now, please!
K.W.

For Luca and Maya
H.A.

Acknowledgements
What Do You Do on a Nature Walk? first published in *A First Poetry Book*, Macmillan Children's Books 2012
If You Were a Giraffe first published in *Bumples* online magazine 2017
Zebra Crossing first published in *Caterpillar* magazine 2015, Crosseros Rhinoceros 2016
Who's the Unclucky One? First published in *Dear Tomato*, ed Carol-Ann Hoyte, 2015
Elephantine Problem, Hippo Hygiene, Hamster on the Loose, originally published as Gerbil on the Loose, first published in *The Dirigible Balloon* 2022
Fox Trot, Albatross first published in *The School Magazine*, Australia 2017
Foal in the Field first published in *Spring*, an online mini-anthology by Brian Moses 2021

Text copyright © Kate Williams 2025
Illustrations copyright © Hannah Asen 2025
First published in Great Britain and in the USA in 2025
by Otter-Barry Books, Little Orchard, Burley Gate,
Herefordshire, HR1 3QS
www.otterbarrybooks.com

All rights reserved

A catalogue record for this book is available from the British Library

Designed by Arianna Osti

ISBN 978-1-915659-55-2

Illustrated with digital media

Set in Minion Pro

Printed in Great Britain

9 8 7 6 5 4 3 2 1

SQUEAK! SQUAWK! ROAR!

Amazing Animal Poems

Poems by
Kate Williams

Illustrations by
Hannah Asen

CONTENTS

Me First!	8
Elephantine Problem	10
If You Were a Giraffe	11
In Memory of Maxie	12
Swanning Along	14
Cow-Calm	16
Woolly but Cool	17
Sunset Bunny Bop	18
Fox Trot	19
Mouse's Houses	20

What Do You Do on a Nature Walk?	22
Hungry Hedgehog	24
Summer Magic	26
Moonpower	28
Sneak, Creep	29
Sing, Sang, Gone	31
Shame about the Voice	32
A Cat's Day In	34
A Dog's View	37
Fishy Wishes	38
Who's the Unclucky One?	40
Secret Pet	41
Smarty Snail	42
Cobra Gets Comfy	43
Crosseros Rhinoceros	44
L-L-L-Look Out!	45

Mothers' Meeting (Kangaroos Only)	47
Elephant	48
Nightfall Fantasy	50
The Wombat is a Non-Bat	51
Exhibit Number 42	52
Chimpantease	53
Sharp-Wrecked	54
Secret Deep	55
Dance of the Penguins	57
While Baby Sleeps	58
Leapfrog	60
Who, Me?	62
Jaguars and Jaguars	64
Hippo Hygiene	67
Zebra Crossing	68
Drifting, Drifting	70
Hamster on the Loose	72
Can't Snap out of It	74
Foal in the Field	76

Pony Friend	79
Zap!	80
Butterfew	82
Vision on the Moor	84
Havoc-Wreakers	85
Albatross	86
Sharky-Lurky	87
Jungle Shrink	88
Mystery Bird	90
What Creature Feature for You?	92
About the poet and the illustrator	94

Me First!

Oh no you don't!
Oh yes I do!
I do want a taste of your strawberry goo.

        Zzzzz

Oh no you won't!
Oh yes I will, or you'll be in for it – hoo-hoo-hoo!

        Zzzzz

No point quibbling – you can't stop me nibbling.
You should say – "Of course, Waspy, do!"

        Zzzzz

I love a picnic tea, and jam especially,
and I can see this spread is meant for me!

        Zzzzz

With apple tart for starters and orange juice for afters,
your basketful will do me splendidly.

Zzzzz

I have my sting with me, so I should just agree,
you shouting, shooing, pesky humans, you!

Zzzzzzzzzzzzzzzzzzzzzzzzzzzzzzzzzzzzzzzzzzzzzz!

Elephantine Problem

Elephants like to look elegant,
but it's hard with all that bulk.
If a giraffe goes gliding past
it puts them in a sulk.

If You Were a Giraffe

If you were a giraffe,
with a drain-long, crane-strong, swing-along neck,
would you just eat leaves?
I wouldn't.
I'd be a spy.

I'd peep over fences ten feet high,
and snoop through windows up in the sky,
and peer into aeroplanes cruising by,
spying all day with my aerial eye
to catch all the crooks and thieves.

Well, I'd do *something* anyway.
I wouldn't just eat leaves.

In Memory of Maxie

Maxie was a short yet very long dog,
short in paw but long as a log.

Springy as a cable and sneakily able,
he could grab a sausage from the kitchen table.

Short in paw but long as a log,
always on the lookout for food to hog,
dinky and slinky, coat all wrinkly,
a sausage-loving, sausage-looking, lovable dog.

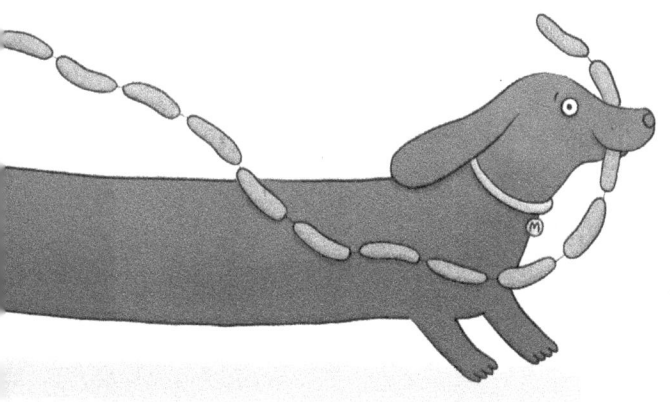

Swanning Along

Swan on the water:
ballet dancer,
tall **S** for Serene,
sending **S**s hooping, looping
far across the sheen.

Swan on the water:
ballet dancer,
S for Statuesque,
going nowhere
slowly, slowly,
still as a statue,
gone.

Cow-Calm

Looking at you, drowsy cows,
peaceful in your sunspot,
I feel peaceful too.

Looking at you, slouchy cows,
comfy in your clover,
I feel comfy too.

Looking at you, dreamy cows,
calm as the meadow grass is green,
casting calmness over the scene,
I feel cow-calm too,
calm as you.

Woolly But Cool

There once was a sheep called Rover
who tired of chewing the clover.
He skipped the stile, strode a mile
and took a world cruise from Dover.

> The rest of his grazing bunch
> paused to goggle, mid-munch.
> *Mad,* they agreed, *daft indeed,*
> and carried on with their lunch.

> > You might catch sight of Rover
> > in the Maldives or Moldova,
> > sat in the sun, enjoying the fun
> > and sampling a peach pavlova.

Sunset Bunny Bop

Spring   down the shady path   *skip, hop*
Dance   through the soft grass   *bop*

Swing   through the cabbages   *skip, hop*
Prance   through the beetroots   *bop*

Bound   through the spooky woods   *skip, hop*
Bounce   round the tree trunks   *bop*

Stop!   Twitchy fox ears!   *Whizz! Hide!*
Pop   down the next hole   *plop*

Fox Trot

Legs in long socks, prancing, prancing,
whiskers bristling, sharp eyes glancing,
tall ears twitching, brush-tail dancing,
coat of fiery red advancing…

Stops, waits.
Something's wrong.
Is the human scent that strong?

Bristle, glance, twitch, dance…

Quick dash –
red flash –
vanish.

Mouse's Houses

Mouse in the meadow – charming sight!
Dainty, dinky little thing!
Peeping out through the primroses.
Aww!

Mouse in the house – alarming sight!
Dirty, stinky little thing!
Peeping out through the cupboard doors.
Aagh!

What Do You Do on a Nature Walk?

We have an adventure, that's what –
crunching through the undergrowth,
dodging thorns and stings,
leaping logs and bridging bogs,
looking out for things:
birds and frogs and shy hedgehogs
and flies with fairy wings
and slimy slugs and tiny bugs –
whatever nature brings!

Hungry Hedgehog

Hedgehog
used to feed in the forest,
but a monster chopped it down.

So hungry hedgehog
foraged in a field,
but a monster sprayed it sour.

So very hungry hedgehog
foraged by the road,
but a monster rush-roared by.

So ravenous hedgehog
foraged in a garden,
but a monster rolled it hard.

So starving hedgehog
squeezed through a hole
and foraged in the wilderness next door.

Contented hedgehog
munched all night
in the cool, fresh dew and the soft moonlight,
curled in a cosy ball at last
and soon fell fast asleep.

Summer Magic

Needle of glass
neon red
flits on lace wings
over pond

Flit-flash-flit
  Flit-flash-flit

Needle of glass
on wings of lace
threading red through
mirrored blue

Abracadazzle

Summer wand

(Red dragonfly)

Moonpower

On my bedroom chair is a tower
of toys and games and books
and sometimes kits or clumps of clay.
That's all
till night.

Then that tower becomes a tiger,
poised, ready to pounce,
glowering through the jungle dark,
fired by a laser beam.

By next day it's gone again
and there's that pile of junk –
the toys and games and books and clay.

Wish I could catch it in between.

Sneak, Creep

Sneak, creep,
tiptoe, creep,
between the screens of
grasses deep,
gold through gold,
black through black,
stripe by stripe
down the streaky track,
sharp-clawed paw
by sharp-clawed paw,
pacing the starlit
jungle floor,
sneak, creep,
tiptoe, creep...
Who's at large,
taking charge
while the reckless
sleep?

(Tiger)

Sing, Sang, Gone

Song thrush singing
in a tree,
how pretty!

Song thrush
in our inner city,
city!

Chainsaw
chopping down the tree,
oh, pity!

Farewell, song thrush
and your ditty,
ditty!

Shame About the Voice

Resplendent is the peacock
with his deep-sea hues –
those gleaming sheens of ocean greens
and shady mauves and blues!

Delicious are his colours,
and how those spots bemuse,
taking the guise of staring eyes
to dazzle and confuse!

Magnetic is the peacock –
he draws a crowd, fair do's!
Vision-wise, he wins first prize.
The shriek, though, he could lose.

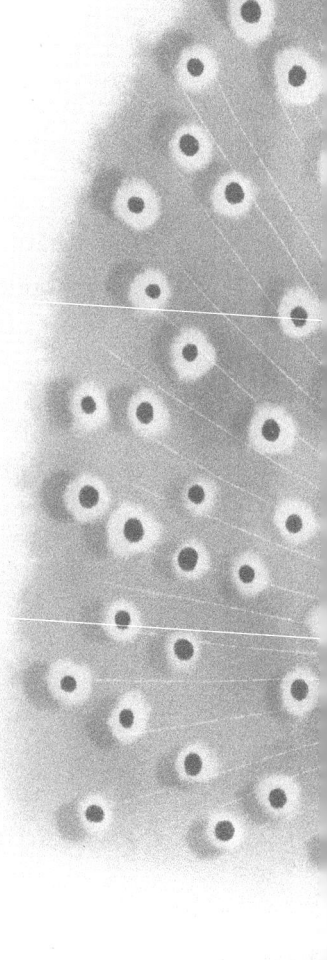

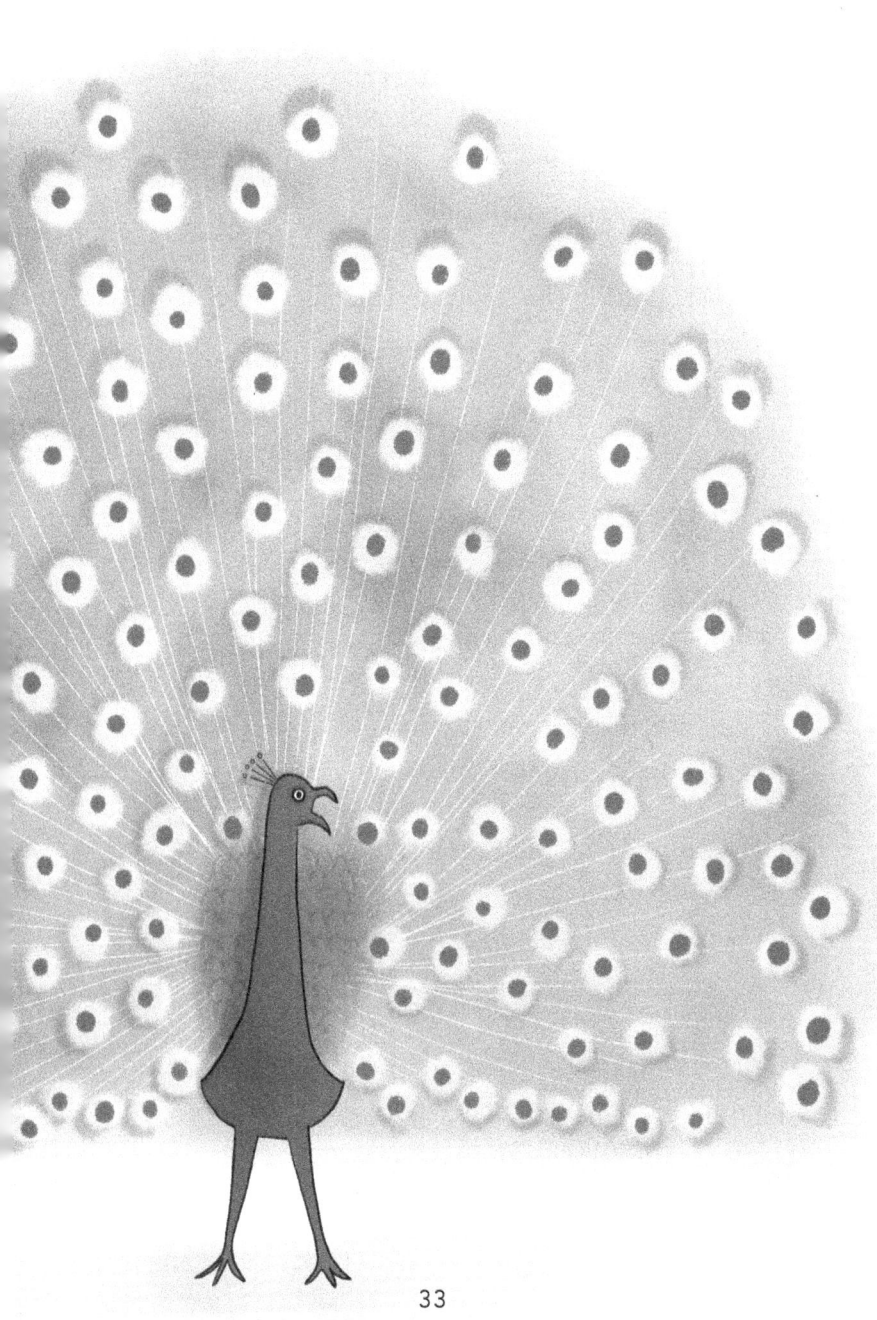

A Cat's Day In

Tiptoe-skip on quilted paws
through the great, tall, open doors.
Twitch of ear,
swish of tail,
yawn,
stretch,
pause.

Where to go? What to do?
Mew of indecision.

Round once more for quick explore:
see what treats may be in store.
Skippetty-quicketty-zippetty-flit –
entertainment mission!

Din-dins dish? No fresh meat.
Window seat? None yet to greet.
Radiator? Not much heat.
Mew of slight vexation.

Zip up to next floor... doors all closed.
Flip-flip down with wrinkled nose.
Ah! New thought begins to call –
sofa relaxation!

Back through hall and great, tall door,
swish-zoom-skid across the floor,
leap up,
curl up,
cuddle up,
snuggle up,
purr, purr, purr...

Purrfection!

A Dog's View

Doggerelly speaking, I can't see the point
of living life like a cat.

Why the washing all day long?
We dogs like to pong!

Why that pussy-footing about?
Want grub? Shout it out!

Why shun your neighbours? Snooty, that!
We like a wee and a chat.

Why the hard stare? Why not a smile?
Why the run-a-cat-mile?

Can't see the point, doggerelly speaking,
of living life like that.

So much merrier to be a bull terrier!
Thank Dog I'm no cat!

Fishy Wishes

I talk to my fish but he can't reply:
underwater, you see.
But he blows me bubbles,
little thought bubbles,
fishy wishes for me.

He'll say *Hey, don't worry!*
or *You'll be just fine!* – plip!
And sometimes he blows rainbows,
or waves his tail – flip!

He sends me fishy wishes,
bubbles just for me,
and I send smiles through the glass,
hoping he can see.

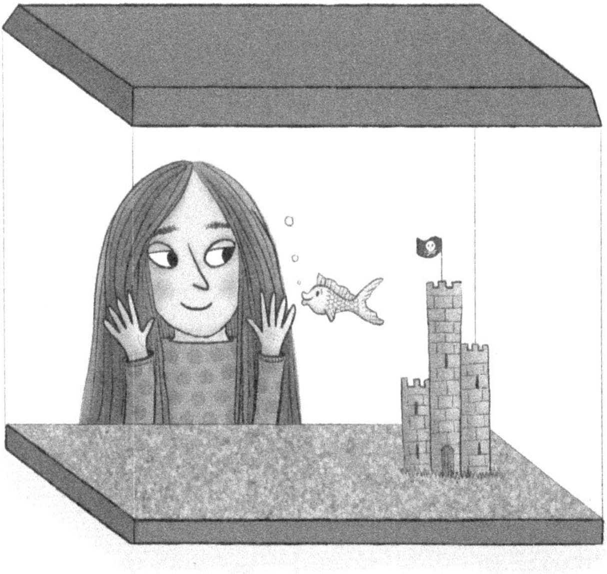

Who's the Unclucky One?

I've no space to spread a wing.
I'm a bird but I don't sing.

I'm barred from the yard, shut up in a cage.
I work all day for no wage.

For meals, I peck at a pile of muck.
No wonder I grumble and cluck!

But I've treats for your tea.
Guess them – and guess me.
You'll find them in shells, in sixes and twelves,
stacked up in boxes on grocery shelves.

So… what wretch could I be?

(A battery hen)

Secret Pet

Dan has a dog. Jake has a cat.
Meg has a rabbit and Ruby's got rats.

My pet is secret – nobody's guessed.
He may be an insect but he's not a pest.

He has no fur, no feathers or scales.
He has no paws, no claws or nails.
He takes no notice of me at all,
even if I beckon, whistle and call.

But at breakfast time, he's sure to be there,
quiet and humble under my chair,
nibbling a fallen orange pip
or cereal crumb or porridge drip.

And nobody knows he's there but me.
After all, a _ _ _ _ louse is quite hard to see.

My pet is secret but maybe you've guessed.
His name is Woody and he is the best!

(Woodlouse)

Smarty Snail

Fancy having a built-in skateboard,
ready-set to ride!
And shelter if it starts to pelter
or you want to hide!

Comfort-roaming, mobile-homing,
sorted from square one!
What oozy-cruisy, lazy-crazy,
saily-snaily fun!

Cobra Gets Comfy

Head
over middle,
top over tip,
wiggle, twiddle,
end-to-end flip,
neck in a huddle,
tum in a cuddle,
throttled, twizzled,
juggled and jigged,
over and under,
almost asunder,
spine in a spiral –
painful? No wonder!
Looped up and cooped up,
tied up and locked,
twisted like ribbon,
tight as a knot.
No room to wriggle,
no space to swivel.
In a slight pickle?
Certainly not!

Crosseros Rhinoceros

Rhinoceros is crosseros:
she'd like to be the boss of us.
If she could choose, *we'd* be in zoos –
or gobbled up like sausageos.

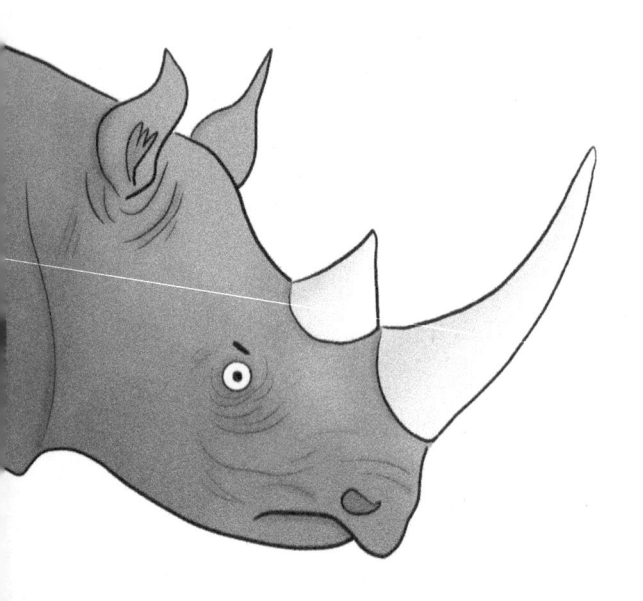

L-L-L-Look Out!

Lazy lion
Lazy lion lounging
Lazy lion lounging in the long grass
Lazy lion lounging in the long grass languidly
Lazy lion lounging in the long grass languidly looking
Lazy lion lounging in the long grass languidly looking at you
Lazy lion lounging in the long grass languidly looking at you
                                        and licking lips

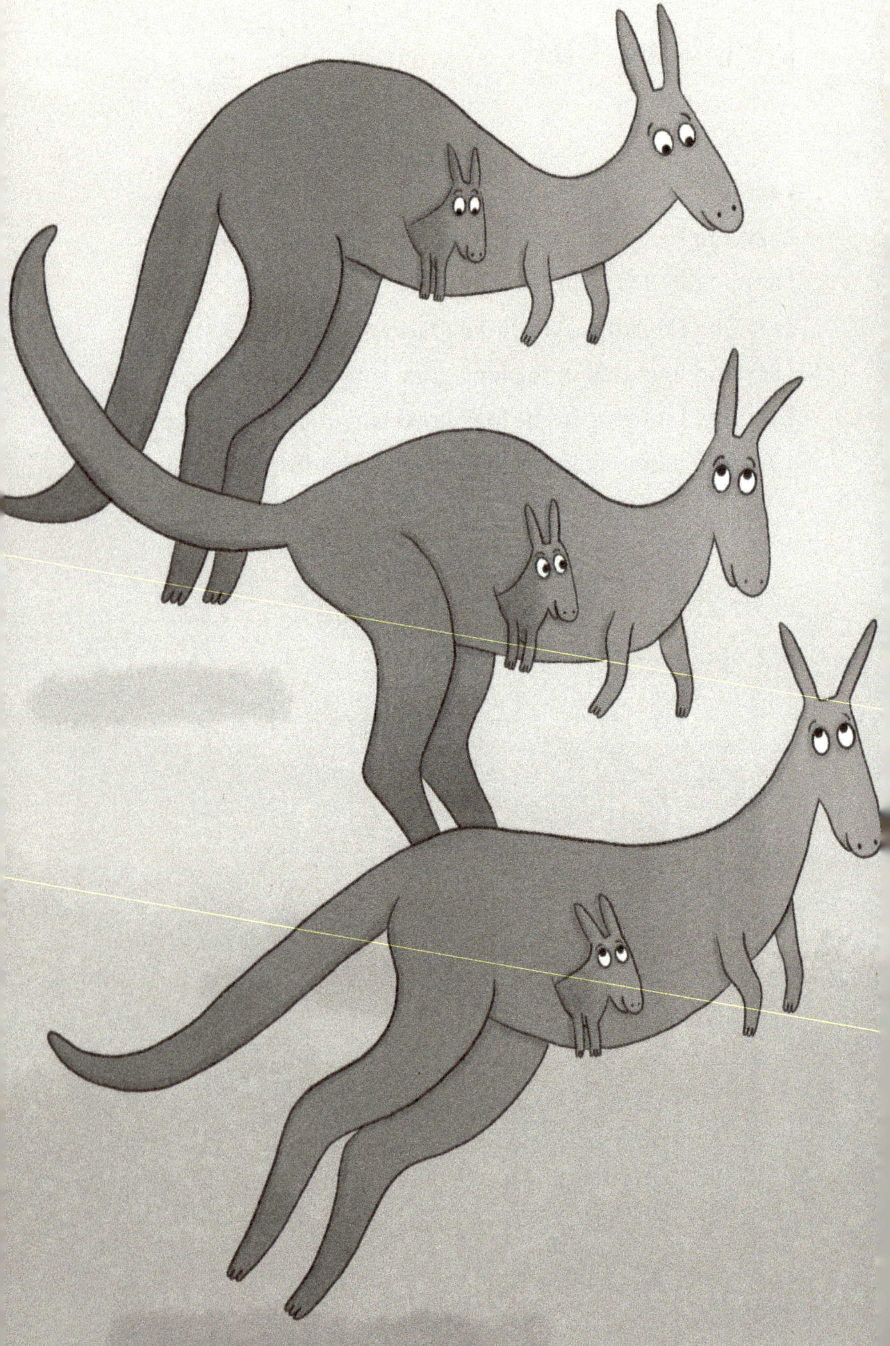

Mothers' Meeting
(Kangaroos Only)

Aren't we lucky, we kangaroo mums,
to have our kiddy pouches built into our tums!

    Poor human beings – they're made all wrong!
    They have to buy a buggy and push it along.

And how it must annoy each human girl and boy
to have to go to school by foot or car or bus!

    Our joeys so enjoy their wobble-tummy run.
    They would never stand for such a silly fuss.

We're blessed to have our pockets
to pop our little poppets
when we go savanna-lollop-hopping.

    Although it must be said that if they walked instead,
    there'd be more room for the shopping!

Elephant

Elephant's tusks are mighty fine.
No wonder he trumpets, *Mine!*
Tusks inherited down the line,
way, way back through time:
great, majestic, ivory curves,
splendid and refined!

Mine! he roars and trumpets, *mine!*
as he tramps the golden grass.
Mine! he bellows, *mine!* he stamps
at any sneaks who pass.

For there are some who seize such gems,
seize and snatch and sell them.

No wonder Elephant blasts away
in the dark of night and dazzle of day
across the vast savannah span:

Mine, mine, MINE!

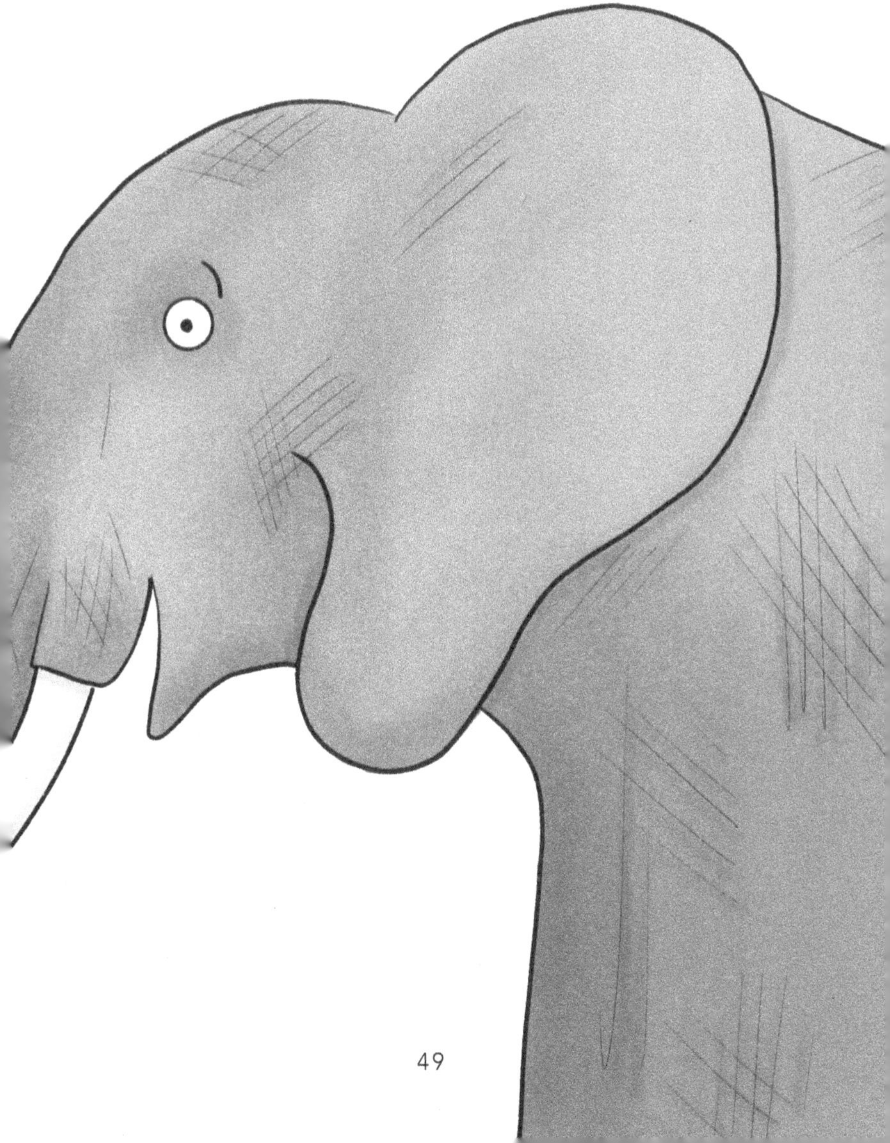

Nightfall Fantasy

Head of mouse,
teeth of rat,
vampire wings
that whip and slap,
eyes that don't see,
ears that do –
donkey's ears that stare at you,
hamster's body,
piglet's nose,
gymnast's legs
that hang from toes,
voice – a pixie's tiny wail,
hobby – night-flight,
fairytale.

(Bat)

The Wombat is a Non-Bat

The wombat is no kind of bat.
He doesn't whizz or flap.
He's short and squat and rather fat,
and does a waddle-pat.

He isn't one to hang from hooks
or anything like that –
he lives a shuffling, snuffling life,
in ground-floor habitat.

No, the wom-'s no flying fruit-,
no night-sky acrobat.
Don't launch him from your starlit roof –
he would just fall flat.

Exhibit Number 42

I'm Exhibit 42,
Cage 3, Block C,
opposite your picnic spot.
That's me.

And you –
tapping my glass,
giving me the shakes,
pointing, waving, peering through,
making faces,
calling your mates –
you're visitor a million,
give one or two.

Hey, let me out! I shout,
but you've already gone,
racing on to 43
or the picnic spot for tea –
racing free.

Chimpantease

If you see a chimpanzee
sitting quietly in a tree,
beware attack!

He may appear quite unaware,
nibbling at some plum or pear,
but mind your...

WHIZZ! Flying banana
　　WHIZZ! Squidgy peach
　　　　WHIZZ! Gooey tomato
　　　　　　WHIZZ! Runny egg

... back!

SMACK!

Sharp-Wrecked

Gentle as the sliding tide is gentle,
peaceful as the lolling waves are peaceful,
rare as her forebears once were plentiful,
harmless as the jagged junk is harmful,
vulnerable as never before,
is turtle.

Secret-Deep

Beneath
our splishing, splashing feet,
below
the waves and boats and ships,
down, down
in the cave-dark deep –
the no-go, no-show, never-know deep,
lurk a shoal of lanternfish,
lit by their own lamp-glow.

Beneath
our splishing, splashing feet,
mystery-deep, secret-deep,
dance a festival of fairy lights,
far,
    far
        below.

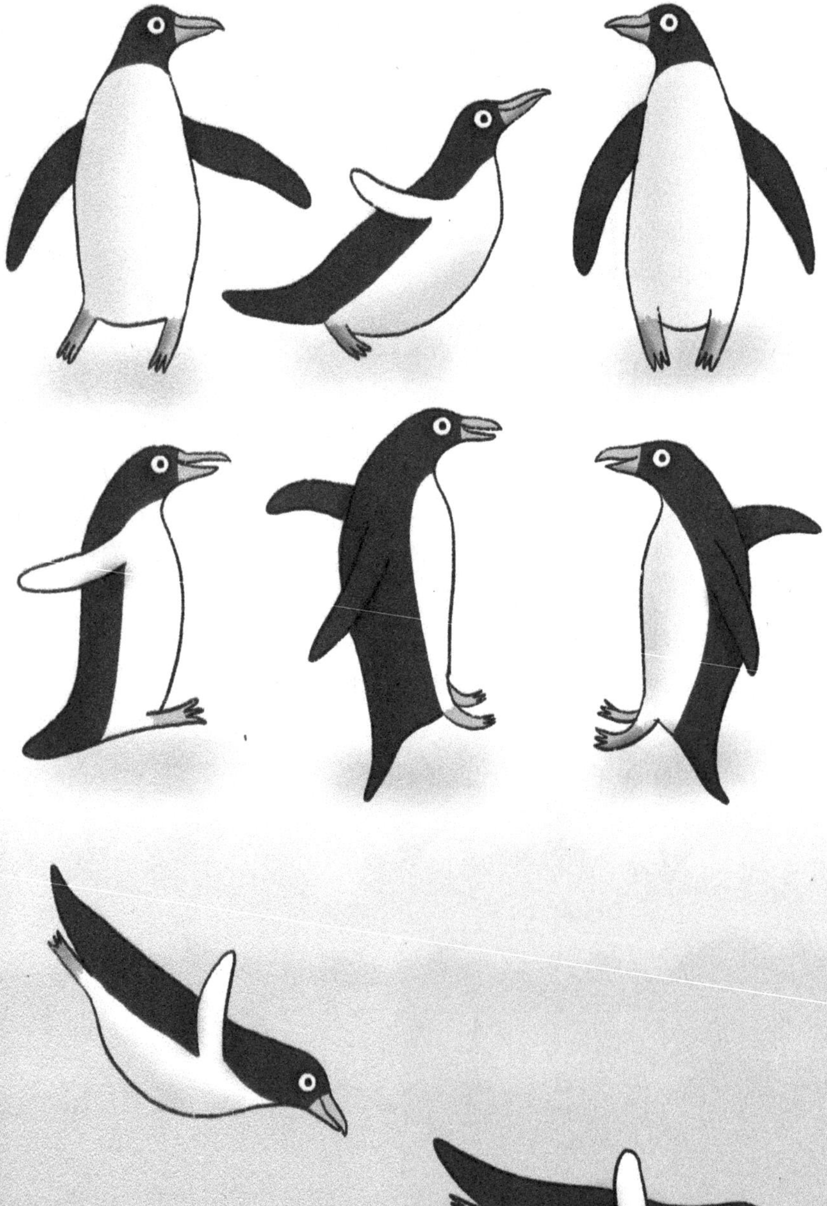

Dance of the Penguins

Step, hop
    waddle, stop
        blink, scratch
            think

Step, hop
    wobble, skid
        dash, splash
            sink

~~~

Sweep, swerve
    steep curve
        diving deep
            jive in perfect sync

While Baby Sleeps

Warm and snug, the newborn cub
twitches a cosy toe,
fast asleep in his bedding heap
of pure, white, Arctic snow.

But the sheet is slipping,
the duvet's dripping,
cracks are appearing below.
Baby bear is unaware,
but Mum knows all about snow.

Warm and snug, the newborn cub
twitches a cosy toe,
sleeping sound while Mum looks round
for a safer place to go.

Leapfrog

Are you good at leapfrog?
Can you *leap-boing* far?
If you were a frog
you'd be a leapfrog star.

With radar eye and elastic thigh,
you'd be springing far and high,
onto the mower as it starts to mow,
in and out of the wheelbarrow,
over the muddy, old ditch below
and across the patch where the parsnips grow,
or – *leap-boing* – over the patio,
skimming the deckchairs set in a row,
up on the sunbed – just for a mo –
and over the washtub you might go,
or across the pond to perch on a rock,
over the lawn and up on a log,
skipping the spade, the fork, the hoe
and the shrubs in the tubs – *leap-boing* – you'd go,

or into the drain and out again,
over the puddle from the overflow,
up the steps in just one go
and over the bluebells – *boing!* – you'd go,
arcing like a rainbow, darting like an arrow,
if only you were a frog.

You'd be a leapfrog super-star
if you were a saggy, baggy, flabby, little

BOING!

garden frog.

Who, Me?

Sometimes I'm a kangaroo,
leaping up and down,
breaking rules and other things,
making people frown.

> Then I'll switch to hedgehog
> and curl up in a ball,
> shut my eyes and stick my spines up,
> hiding from them all.

Usually then I count to ten
and uncurl as a bunny,
skipping, playing with my friends,
super-sweet as honey.

> Once I was a lion,
> once a biting snake –
> can't remember why I was,
> probably by mistake.

Right now I'm myself –
bits of everything,
just enough of kangaroo
to help the fun to swing.

Jaguars and Jaguars

People think I have four wheels,
and another one, too, to sit behind.
They think I go *brmm, brmm, toot, toot!*
But they'll find,
should they meet me one dark night,
that I'm a jag of a junglier kind –
not that *I'd* mind,
but *they* might.

65

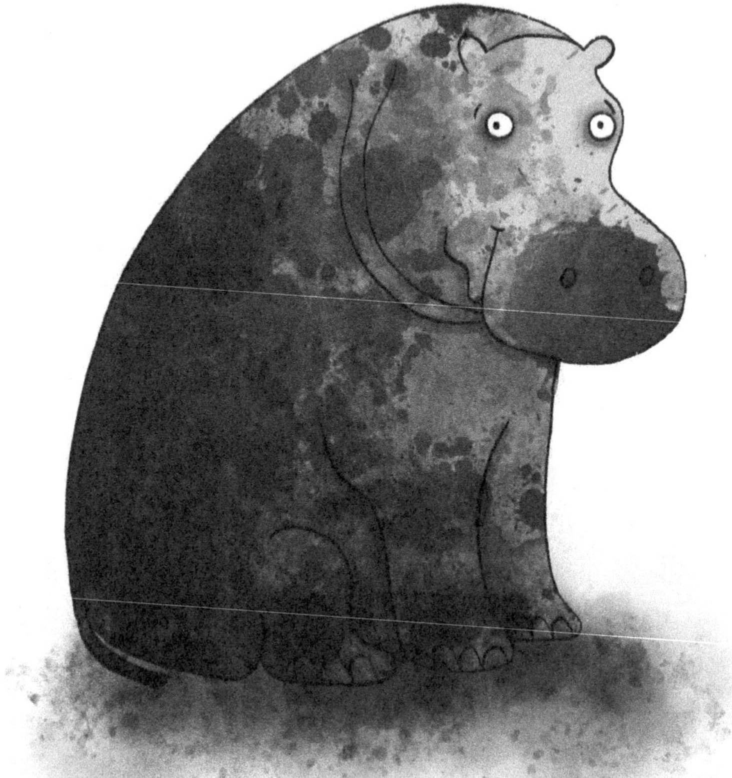

Hippo Hygiene

Hippo's not keen on getting clean.
He'd rather smell.

He loves his squelchy, muddy gunge,
so save your shower gel and sponge.
Never mind what's right or wrong.
He'd rather pong.

No, don't bother with the hose.
Leave him soaking to his nose.
Never mind what people think.
He'd rather stink.

Let him do what hippos do –
semi-sink in gorgeous goo.
A little dirt won't hurt,
so leave him, do!

And forget the clean shirt.

Zebra Crossing

Nobody saw
the zebra crossing,
slow, stately, large.

Nobody spotted
the stripes on the crossing –
lost in camouflage.

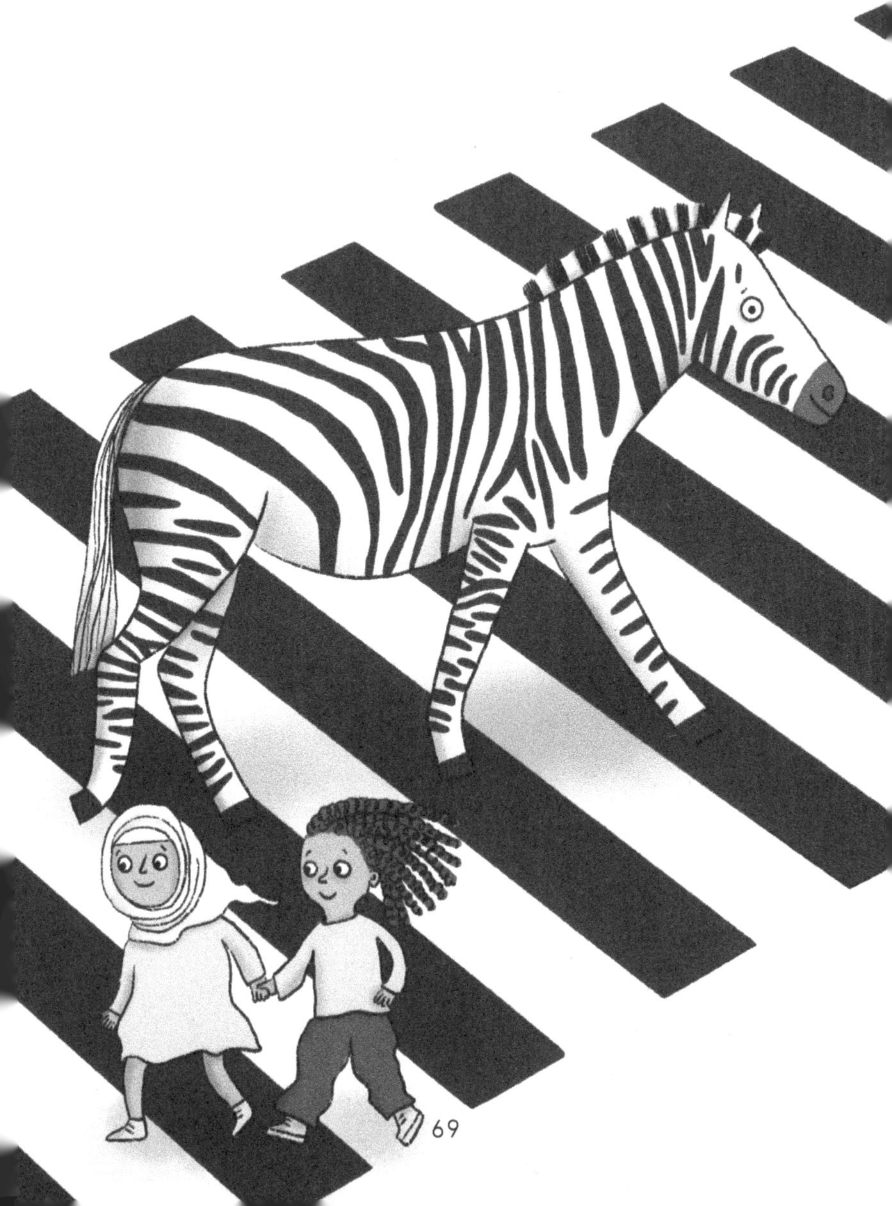

Drifting, Drifting

Drifting through the air,
   legs a-dangle,
      skirting nettles, gorse, brambles,
         just drifting.

Drifting in your path,
   legs a-tangle,
      brushing your knee, elbow, hair,
         just drifting.

Silver-grey as the evening light,
   half in, half out of sight,
      thread-legs, web-wings, pin-thin body,
         just drifting.

You can wave,
> clap,
> sing,
> shout,
> swing
> your arms about...

but the daddy-longlegs
   has never a care,
      a-sail in the fairytale August air,

         just drifting.

Hamster on the Loose

Let your hamster out and it may
hop it before you can stop it –

roll in a ball
and spin down the hall

hide in a shoe
pop to the loo

devour a box
of exquisite chocs

gobble a carrot
bother the parrot

bathe in the flour
take a hot shower

try your computer
borrow your scooter

head out the door
leave to explore

or just curl up in your pocket

Can't Snap out of It

I'm at the dentist's
– *Oo-ee-ah!*
about to have a filling
– *Oo-ee-ah!*
I've promised not to bite
– *Oo-ee-ah!*
when he starts the drilling
– *Oo-ee-ah!*

But biting's what I do
– *Snap-snap-snap!*
I'm that type of reptile
– *Snap-snap-snap!*
So it's tricky not to
– *Snap-snap-stop!*
and drilling's not my style
– *Snap-snap-strop!*

I've got a rotten tooth
– *Rot-rot-rot*
ruining my smile
– *Blot-blot-blot*

Bite him I must not
– *Not-not-not*
or he'll run a mile
– *Non-stop-rot*

Oopsy! I just did
– *Snap-snap-forgot!*
Dentist's run and hid
– *Now-snap-what?*

Zero fang repair
– *Oh-snap-no!*
Smileo despair
– *Oh-snap-woe!*

Dental care's a nightmare
an anti-gnasher bitemare
an impossidrillity
for a

croc-*snap*-o-*snap*-dile!

Foal in the Field

Foal in the field
lazing, dozing:
bundle in the buttercup grass.

Foal in the field
rolling, playing:
fun-lover in the warm sun.

Foal in the field
rising, wobbling:
stilt-walker having a go.

Foal in the field
skipping, gliding:
dancer in a gold glow.

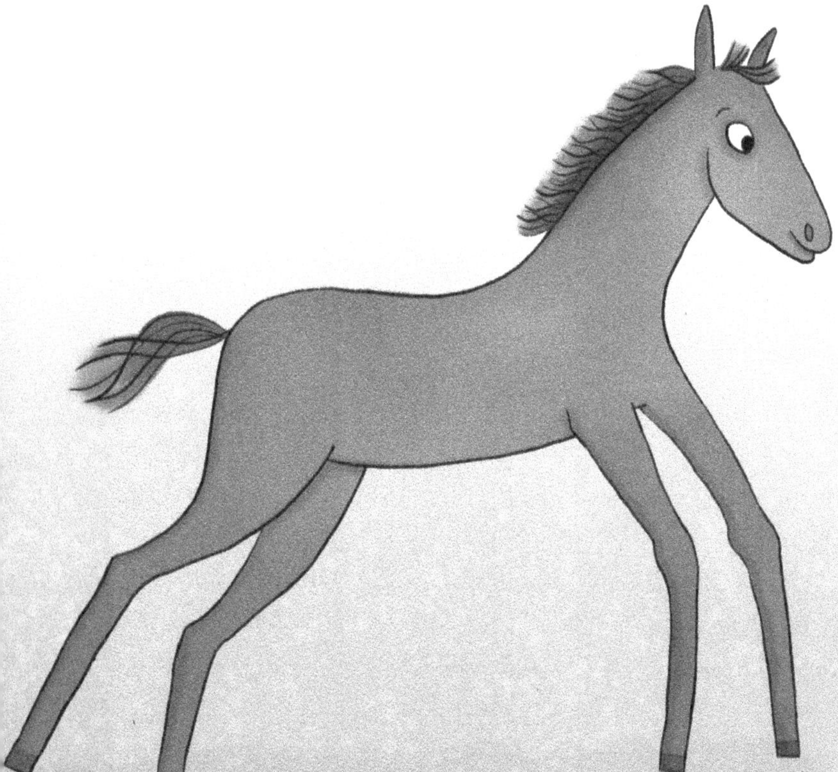

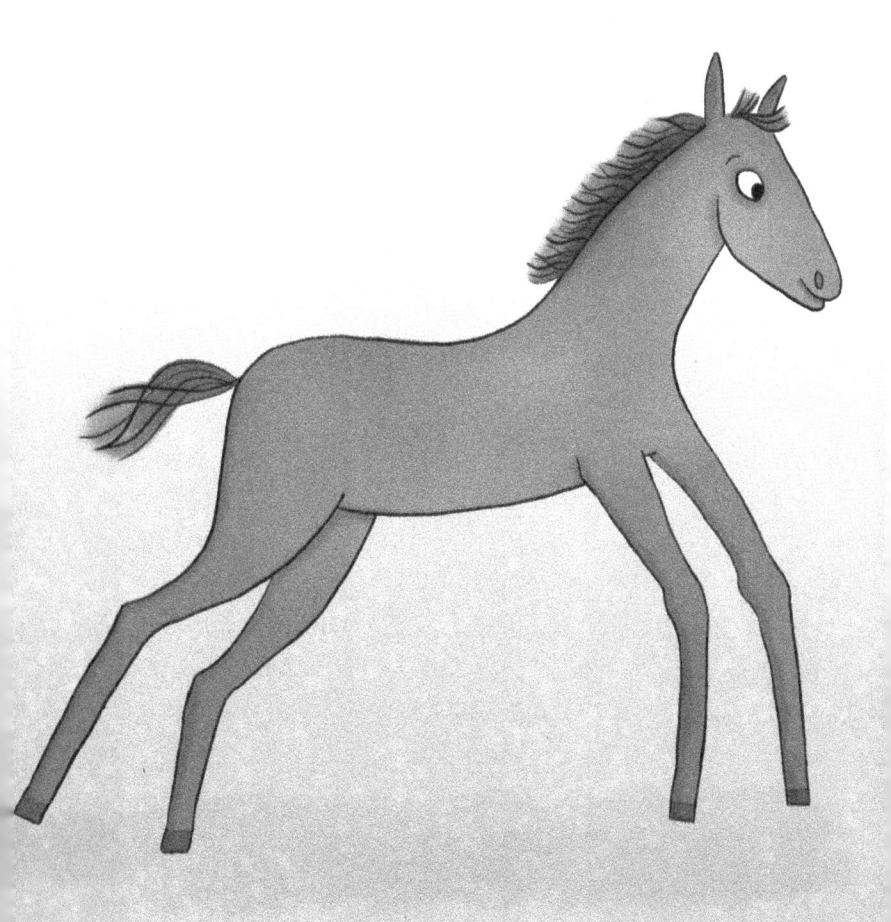

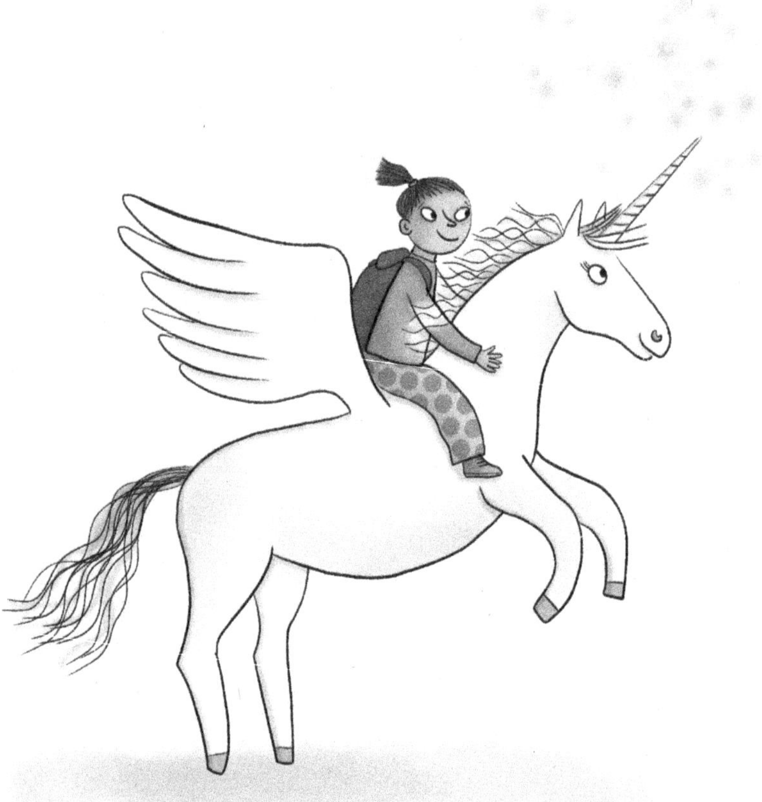

Pony Friend

Ruth says *Walk!*
and Pony walks.

Ruth says *Stop!*
and he stops.

She says *Canter! Gallop! Jump!*
and Pony will obey.

She strokes his soft, smooth, velvet fur
and knows he feels her care.

She breathes the warming, soothing bond
that she and Pony share.

Sometimes he's a unicorn, flying her to school,
or a mascot in her pocket, or her prince.

Other people may not see him,
or not every day,
but for Ruth, Ruth alone,
Pony's always there.

Zap!

You won't see squirrels strolling,
donned in scarf and cap,
step by step, enjoying the scene…
They just *zap!*

Vertically, up the tallest tree –
no safety rope or strap,
no climbing boots, no parachutes –
just *zap!*

They never check the updates
on their squirrel app,
nor the forest weather forecast –
let alone a map.

Owl in hollow? Cat below?
Twig about to snap?
Nothing ever stops a squirrel –
unless a nut to tap.

Traffic laws for speeding paws?
Hidden camera trap?
Caution? Slow? *Squirrels?* No!
Wiggle-wriggle-flip-flap –

Z – A – P !

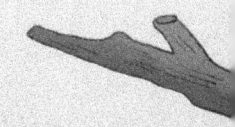

Butterfew

Butterfly
    satin bow, pansy-pretty, smile-bright

  Butterhue
      dreamy blue, silky orange, creamy white

    Buttershy
        flower-gentle, petal-frail, leafy-light

      Butterfew
          far too few, flicker-slip, out of sight

83

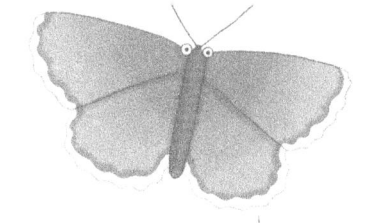

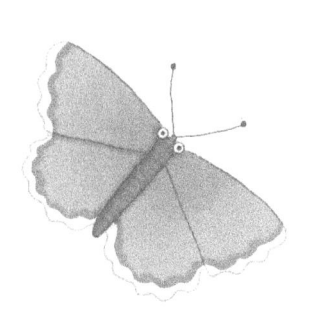

A Vision on the Moor

Like paper cut-outs,
the red deer pose,
sun-lit, prop-still
between the dark hills
till,
soundless as feathers, they flit-flit-flit,
riding the stage on fairy tiptoes.

In their spotlight
the red deer dance,
then,
sprite-light, skip to the wings,
blending with the heather,
melding with the moor,
melting into the shadows.

Havoc-Wreakers

Cliff-sweepers
surf-scrapers
squawk-shriekers
peace-breakers

beach-sneakers
snack-raiders
picnic-eaters
devastators

Albatross

Lone ocean bird
        surfing the sunset's glow –
                      so bright, so white
                so graceful, so grand
        so calm
      so strong
    solo

Sharky-Lurky

In the darky-murky, sharky-lurky sea,
a meany, mighty beasty there could be,
seeing what his swivel eye can see
for munchy-crunchy breakfast, lunch and tea.

If such a meany beasty there should be,
leering at you with a look of glee,
humming – *Yummy num-nums, all for me!* –
then

flee, flee, flee!

Jungle Shrink

Brmmm-thud! Brmmm-thud!

The roars are nearing.
The sky's gaping in.
There's a great hole letting in the light.

The jaguar feels cornered.
The viper's curled up tight.
The tree-top monkey's watching out.
The eagle's raised her height.

Brmmm-thud! Brmmm-thud!
Something isn't right.

The leopard wobbles on his branch.
The poisonous frog takes fright.
The parrot turns her squawking down
and curbs her flouncy flight.

The wide-eyed lemur squints and blinks.
The spider holds her bite.
The sloth in his cosy sun-lounge shivers.
Chameleon turns white.

"Our jungle is shrinking!"
the creatures are thinking.

Brmmm-brmmm-thud!
And they think right.

Mystery Bird

I've the grace of an angel, the whiteness of snow,
and I inspire peace wherever I go.

I'm cousin to pigeon, I have to confess,
but *I* wouldn't splatter your town with mess!

I like to reside in the countryside
where cattle can graze and herons can glide.

I float and flutter and sail above,
and rhyme with a word you're sure to **love**.

(Dove)

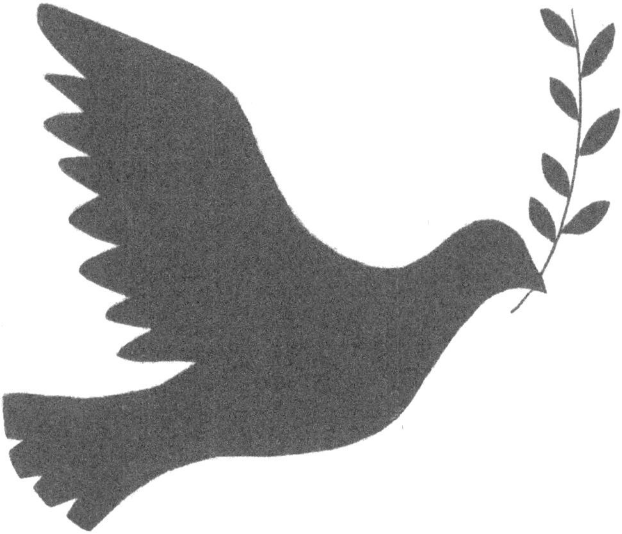

What Creature Feature for You?

If you could acquire, for a quarter of an hour,
any animal feature,
what speciality would you pick
from all the plethora?

A tail? A beak? A roar? A squeak?
Iridescent scales? Penguin feet?
A cheetah's speed? A sloth's relax?
A hamster's pouch for secret snacks?
A blackbird's song? A screech owl's shriek?
A gerbil's shy? A chimp's bold cheek?
Flies' eyes, bees' knees, grasshopper clicks?
Chameleon's crafty colour-change tricks?
A dolphin's charms? An octopus's arms?
A duck-billed platypus's muddled-up mix?

What creature feature would you pick,
just for a quarter of an hour?

Nothing? Not a farmyard moo?
A fine set of fangs? A pong from the zoo?
Zilch? Zero?
Quite right too!

You're perfect as you are.

KATE WILLIAMS

spent her childhood in London, next door to a cat,
a tortoise and some terrapins. She later moved to
Bristol – in earshot of the zoo – and now lives in the
rolling farmland of Wales, surrounded by baas, moos
and cock-a-doodle-doos. She meets some interesting
creatures on her school poetry visits, too. Snakes in a
classroom? Quite normal. Kate is in her top comfort
zone when crafting poems for young readers
and listeners. Her poetry has contributed to numerous
children's anthologies, with publishers such as
Macmillan, Bloomsbury, Hodder, Dorling Kindersley
and Oxford University Press.

More on her website: **katewilliamspoet.com**

HANNAH ASEN

is a freelance illustrator based in Scotland.
She specialises in creating vibrant illustrations and
unique commissions for clients worldwide. Originally
from London, Hannah's love for illustration was ignited
during her time in the creative hub of Berlin, where she
immersed herself in the dynamic artistic community
and decided to pursue her passion as a career. Recently,
she has embraced the tranquillity of the East Lothian
countryside, drawing from the beautiful natural
surroundings, and continues to bring her imaginative
visions to life through her art. *Squeak! Squawk! Roar!* is
Hannah's second book for Otter-Barry Books, following
Chicken on the Roof by Matt Goodfellow.